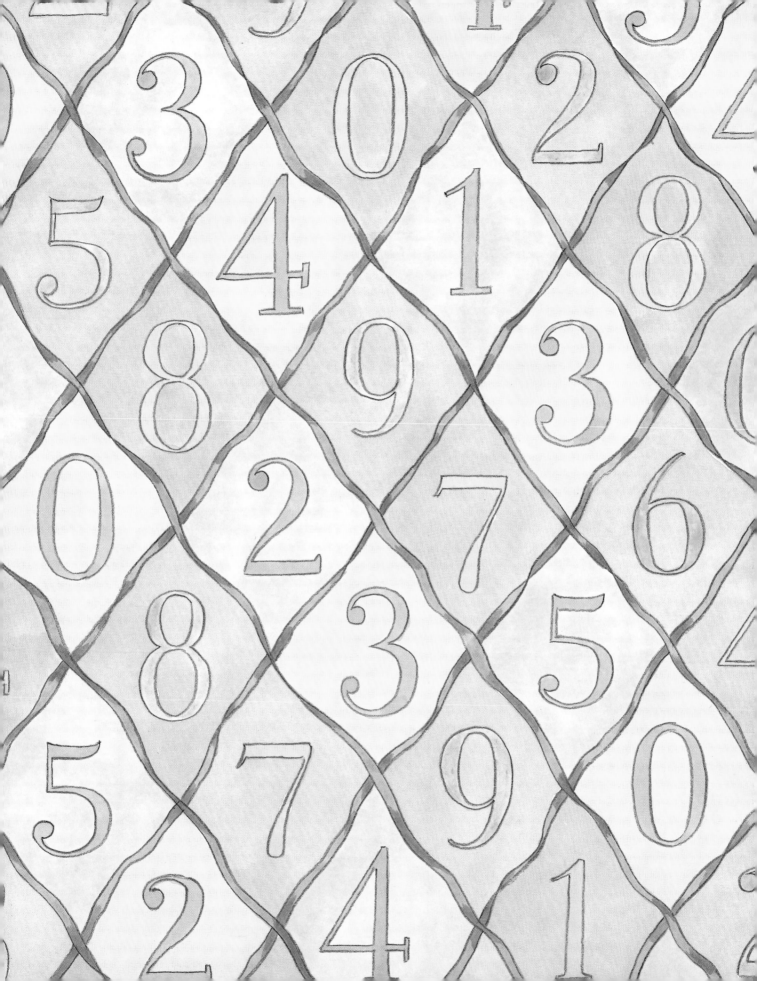

for Ottoline

A Doubleday Book for Young Readers

Published by
Bantam Doubleday Dell Publishing Group, Inc.
1540 Broadway
New York, New York 10036

Doubleday and the portrayal of an anchor with a dolphin are trademarks of
Bantam Doubleday Dell Publishing Group, Inc.

Copyright © 1997 by Emma Chichester Clark
First American edition 1997
Originally published in Great Britain by Andersen Press Ltd.

ISBN: 0-385-32517-7
Cataloging-in-Publication Data is available from the U.S. Library of Congress.

The text of this book is set in 15-point Goudy.

Manufactured in Italy

October 1997

10 9 8 7 6 5 4 3 2 1

Little Miss Muffet's COUNT-ALONG SURPRISE

Emma Chichester Clark

A Doubleday Book for Young Readers

Little Miss Muffet
Sat on a tuffet,
Eating her curds and whey;
There came a big spider,
Who sat down beside her
And frightened Miss Muffet away.

Traditional nursery rhyme

1

Little Miss Muffet
Sat on a tuffet,
Eating her curds and whey,
When along came one spider
Who sat down beside her,
And said to Miss Muffet,
"Please stay!"

Little Miss Muffet
Sat on the tuffet,
Eating her curds and whey,
When along came two Lemurs
With trumpets and streamers,
And bunting to make a display.

Little Miss Muffet
Sat on the tuffet,
Eating her curds and whey,
When along came three magpies
With taffeta bow ties,
And silk vests of very pale gray.

Little Miss Muffet
Sat on the tuffet,
Eating her curds and whey,
When along came four foxes
With neatly wrapped boxes,
And Jell-O lined up on a sleigh.

Little Miss Muffet
Sat on the tuffet,
Eating her curds and whey,
When along came five pussycats
With milk shakes and party hats,
And small pots of chocolate soufflé.

Little Miss Muffet
Sat on the tuffet,
Eating her curds and whey,
When along came six poodles
With oodles of noodles,
And flutes, which they started to play.

Little Miss Muffet
Sat on the tuffet,
Eating her curds and whey,
When along came seven bears
With a table and chairs.
They said, "We'll sit here, if we may."

Little Miss Muffet
Sat on the tuffet,
Eating her curds and whey,
When along came eight puffins
With blueberry muffins,
And each clutched a tiny bouquet.

Little Miss Muffet
Sat on the tuffet,
Eating her curds and whey,
When along came nine gibbons
With balloons tied with ribbons,
And bananas arranged on a tray.

Little Miss Muffet
Sat on the tuffet,
Eating her curds and whey,
When along came ten crocodiles
With a box and ten greedy smiles.
They saw her and shouted, "HOORAY!"

Little Miss Muffet
Jumped up from her tuffet,
And looked at the box in dismay.
Were they taking her back
In a box as a snack?
But she waited to hear what they'd say.

AND...

There was cheering and prancing,
And whooping and dancing–
And what did the crocodiles say?
"You have made a mistake;
We have brought you a cake!
Don't you know? It's your birthday today!"

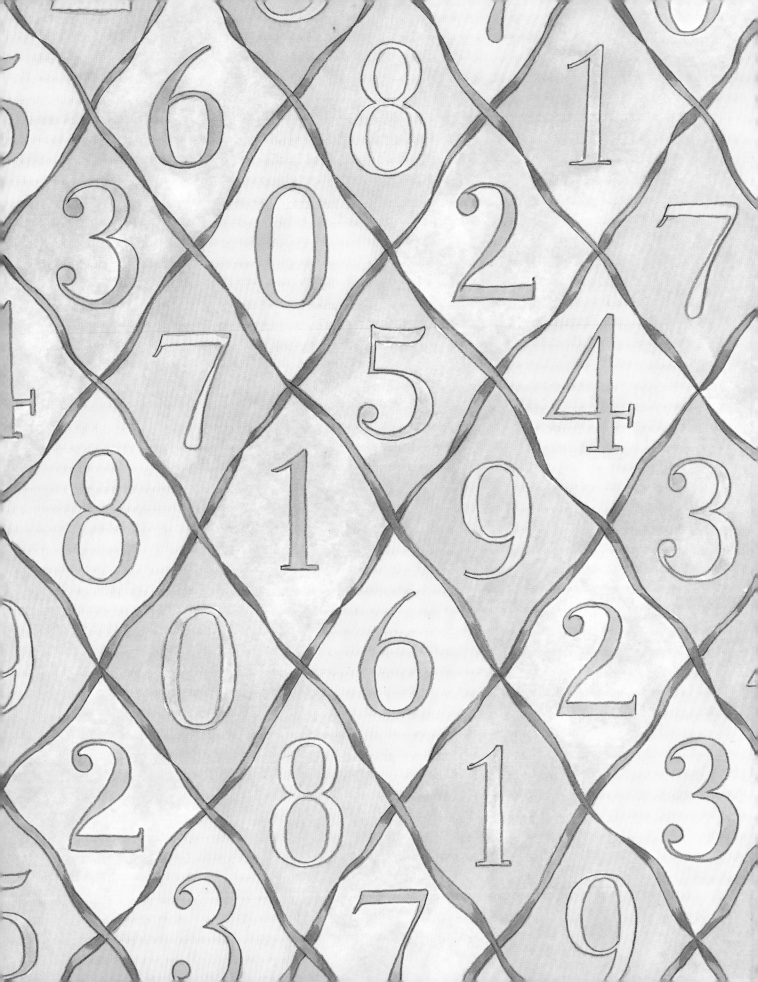